Dora's Costume Party

by Christine Ricci
illustrated by Zina Saunders

Jaden
Thompson
Chhael
OThrr

Published by Advance Publishers, L.C.
Maitland, FL 32751 USA
www.advancepublishers.com
Produced by Judy O Productions, Inc.
Designed by SunDried Penguin

Printed in China

ISBN 1-57973-308-5

¡Hola! I'm Dora! Today is Halloween. My favorite thing about Halloween is getting dressed up in a costume. We're having a Halloween costume party at my house, and everyone is getting ready. But Boots can't decide what costume to wear.

Boots might want to dress up as a superhero who rescues anyone who needs help. Or he could be a baseball player who can hit the ball over the fence and win the game!

Or maybe he'll be a clown who does tricks in the circus. Boots can't decide, and it's almost time for the party!

Look! There's Tico! Do you know what Tico wants to be for Halloween? Yeah, a cowboy! Tico is pretending that he's a cowboy who rides a horse through the desert! Wow! What a great costume!

But Tico is missing part of his costume. Let's help him look in the costume box. Do you see a cowboy hat? Now we just need to find a star badge. Great! Tico's costume is finished. We'll see Tico at the party.

Benny's still working on his costume too. What do you think Benny wants to be for Halloween? *Sí,* a slice of pizza! That's a really yummy costume idea. Benny's favorite kind of pizza has pepperoni, peppers, and cheese on it! But he needs help to put these ingredients on his pizza costume. Will you help?

Benny can use red circles for pepperoni. Let's look for five red circles. The green squares look like peppers. Will you find four green squares for him? And the yellow rectangles can be cheese. Do you see eight yellow rectangles? *¡Excelente!* Thanks for helping Benny get his costume ready!

Guess what Isa wants to be for Halloween. Isa's going to be the most graceful ballerina ever! She'll use her ballet slippers to stand on her tiptoes, twirl around, and jump in the air.

But where are her ballet slippers? Do you see them?

There's my cousin Diego. He's going to dress up like a deep-sea diver. A deep-sea diver explores the ocean looking at fish and animals. Diego already has on his special diving suit, but he still needs to find his flippers and a swimming mask. Do you see them?

Seeing all these great costumes gave Boots an idea for his Halloween costume. But it's a surprise! Boots promises that we'll see his Halloween costume at the party. *¡Vámonos!* We're almost at my house!

Look! My baby sister and brother are dressed in their costumes.

Can you guess what my baby sister is for Halloween? *Sí, una fresa.* Strawberries are her favorite fruit!

Can you guess what my baby brother's costume is?
Yes, he's dressed as *las uvas*. He loves grapes.

The babies are so cute in their costumes! Now it's my turn to get ready. I'm wearing a flower costume. But my costume is missing two petals. To figure out where the missing ones go, let's look at the colors of the petals: yellow, red, orange.

It's a pattern. Do you see where the red petal belongs? Where does the orange petal go?

Let's decorate *mi casa*! First *Papi* needs help with the cake. Will you find two triangles for the pumpkin's eyes? *¡Gracias!* *Abuela* needs help finding the balloons. Do you see five orange balloons? Let's count them in Spanish. *¡Uno, dos, tres, cuatro, cinco!* Now, let's help *Mami* look for ten apples to go inside the ten goody bags!

Oh! I think I hear someone at the door.

The guests are here! There's Isa, the graceful ballerina. Tico, the cowboy, is riding his trusty horse. Benny's pizza costume looks delicious! And Diego really looks like a deep-sea diver.

But I don't see Boots.
I wonder where he is.

Here he is! But what is Boots's Halloween costume?

Oooooh! Boots couldn't decide on just one thing for his Halloween costume. So he decided to wear all of his favorite costumes.

He's a superhero-baseball player-clown! What a cool costume!

Everyone has such great Halloween costumes. Thanks for helping us get ready for the party. We did it! Happy Halloween!